MY FRIEND MAC

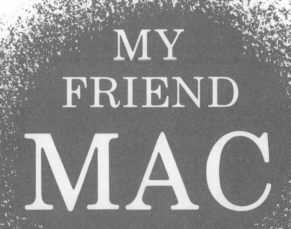

MY
FRIEND
MAC

THE STORY OF LITTLE BAPTISTE AND THE MOOSE

by MAY McNEER & LYND WARD

Houghton Mifflin Company Boston
The Riverside Press Cambridge

Fourth Printing   w

Deep in the woods, a long way from St.
Michel village, lived Little Baptiste. He
lived with his mother, Big Marie, and his
father, Big Baptiste. There were no other
houses near Little Baptiste's home, so he
had no one to play with. Sometimes he
was very lonely.

"Will you take me fishing?" Little Baptiste said to his father one day.

"I have to plow the big field. I can't go fishing," said Big Baptiste. "I wish I could go with you. I used to go fishing with my friend Mac. He was a real fisherman. Mac used to catch the biggest fish in the lake. You will have to go fishing alone, Little Baptiste."

Then Little Baptiste went to his mother. "Will you play hide-and-seek with me?" he asked her.

"I have no time for games today," said Big Marie. "I must wash the clothes. Your father used to play games with his good friend, Mac, and run races, too.

"Perhaps sometime your father will play hide-and-seek with you, when his work is done."

Little Baptiste found his father working in the field. He said, "Tell me about your friend Mac. Did you play games with him?"

Big Baptiste stopped work and said, "I wish you had a friend like Mac. He had big feet. He had a great big nose. He wasn't pretty, no? But he could slide in the snow. He could pick berries. Mac was good at playing games too."

Little Baptiste said sadly, "I have no brothers and sisters. My mother had seven brothers and six sisters. She wasn't lonely, no? My father had four brothers and five sisters. And he had a friend named Mac. I do not even have a friend."

Then he said, "I'll go out and look for a friend."

So he put two cookies into his pocket and he set out down the road. Soon he saw a trail going to the deep woods. His shoes made a wet sound on the trail. A snowbird flew up. Little Baptiste said, "Goodbye, snowbird. Come back next year, when the cold wind blows."

Little Baptiste walked and walked. He didn't come to a farm.

"I'll go back home," he said at last. He looked for the trail but he couldn't find it.

It was getting late. The woods were dim. Little Baptiste sat down on a stump and tried not to cry.

Behind the stump he heard a little
sound. He was afraid that it might be a
big black bear, ready to eat him. He
turned around. There was a funny, ugly
calf with a big nose.

"I know what you are. You are a baby
moose," said Little Baptiste. "Where
is your mother?"

He went to the baby moose. It put out its wet tongue and licked his face. Little Baptiste sat down beside it.

The woods were darker now. Little Baptiste put his arm around the moose calf. He tried not to be afraid. Then, away in the dim trees he saw a little light. It winked up and down as it came closer. He could hear his father shout, "Little Baptiste! Where are you?"

"Here I am. Right here."

Big Baptiste came running and picked him up. They went home. The baby moose followed them on its long, wobbly legs.

At the farm the baby moose came right into the open door of the house. When Big Marie saw Little Baptiste she was happy. When she saw the moose she was surprised. She said, "Bless me! What is that?"

Little Baptiste said, "This is my friend Mac."

His mother and his father laughed. His father said, "My friend Mac was not very pretty. Very ugly he was, yes? But he was not as ugly as this Mac."

"I don't care," said Little Baptiste. "Mac is my friend."

Mac was happy in his bed behind the
stove. He liked his new home very much.
He was curious about everything in the
farmyard. He ran after the puppy. He
met the pig. He surprised the goat.
Mac wanted to play, too. The cat didn't
like to play with him. She wanted to be
anywhere but where Mac was.

Little Baptiste tried and tried to teach Mac how to be a good pet. He couldn't seem to teach him. Mac wanted to eat with the family at the table. Little Baptiste said, "No, Mac, you can't. Go outside and eat from your own dish."

Mac came to eat with them anyway.

"My friend didn't have very good manners. But he never tipped the table over on the floor," said Big Baptiste.

Big Marie was angry. She flapped her apron at Mac. She clapped her hands at him. She shook the broom in front of his big nose.

"He butts with his head! He pounds with his feet! He sits on my bread," she shouted.

Little Baptiste put his arm around Mac. He said, "He is my friend."

Big Baptiste said with a frown, "Mac is not polite. He cannot live in the house."

Little Baptiste made up a bed for Mac in the shed. Soon Mac was eating from a big pail some of the time. Best of all he liked to eat the green branches of Big Marie's peach tree.

"That Mac!" said Big Marie. "We will have no peaches this summer."

In summer Mac came by each morning
to waken Little Baptiste. He pulled up
the latch with his teeth. Then he walked
right into the house and into the room
where Little Baptiste was asleep.

They played hide-and-seek in the
farmyard. Mac didn't hide very well.
Little Baptiste thought that he didn't
like to play games so much, after all.

He took Mac to the garden to help pick berries. "You must help me work, you know, Mac," said Little Baptiste. "When we have picked the berries we will find the eggs in the straw."

Big Baptiste went to the garden. He pulled on his beard. He shouted, "Little Baptiste, your not-so-pretty friend has picked the berries, yes? He has pulled up all of the bushes, too!"

Little Baptiste went into the hen house and found six eggs. But Mac tried to follow him, and he got stuck in the door. The silly hens clucked and flew about in fright. Straw went every which way!

One day Little Baptiste told his mother,
"Mac and I are going fishing. We will
catch the biggest fish in the lake."

When they came to the lake shore he
said to Mac, "Now, you sit down beside
me. Do not make a sound, or you will
keep that big fish away."

Then Mac saw some lily pads floating near the shore. He waded out in the water and began to eat them. A moose likes lily pads better than anything else. The thump-thump sound that he made sent the fish to hide in deep water.

"You and your big feet!" said Little Baptiste as he started home.

"Mac isn't good at fishing," said Little Baptiste. "Just the same he is my friend. We can do other things."

Big Baptiste shook his head. "Mac is a moose," he said. "He looks like a moose. He acts like a moose."

When the cold wind whistled around his ears, and the snowbird came back, Little Baptiste got out his sled. He called to Mac, "The most fun of anything is to slide downhill on the snow. Come with me. I will show you how."

Mac went along, but he didn't learn to slide very well.

Soon Mac was too big for the shed. He went to live in the field. The snow had gone, and the trees were green. Little Baptiste talked things over with Mac.

"Mac," he asked, "why don't you do things right? I try to teach you the right way. My mother told me to wipe my feet when I come in the house. You don't wipe yours. Now my mother won't let you in the house any more.

"There is only one thing you do well. You can run fast. I think you could run faster than a monkey or a kangaroo!"

Mac thrust his big nose at Little Baptiste, and pushed him over.

"Well, I guess that means you think so too," said Little Baptiste, dusting himself off. "Next time just nod your head a little bit."

"If I am to keep up with you now," said Little Baptiste, "I think I will have to ride."

So he got up on Mac's back and shouted, "Let's go, Mac!"

Mac began to walk around the field. Then he trotted along the road. Then he ran faster and faster. Little Baptiste had to hold on with both arms and both legs. The wind hit his face. It whistled in his ear.

Little Baptiste began to laugh and to shout, "I'm having fun. I'm having fun. Run, Mac, run!"

They stopped to see some men at work
putting up a house.

"What do you think they are up to,
Mac?" asked Little Baptiste. Then Little
Baptiste and Mac went racing home.

When the trees began to glow with red and gold, Mac started to do strange things. Little horns came out of his head.

"They feel like fur," said Little Baptiste.

Mac liked to bump them on stumps. He pawed with his feet in the dust.

"You never did things like this before. What has happened, Mac?" asked Little Baptiste. Mac had taken to going deep into the woods alone.

"Why do you go away, Mac? Why don't you let me ride while you race down the road?"

His mother and father were sad, watching Little Baptiste go to look for Mac in the woods.

"Come here, my little son," said Big
Baptiste, setting him on his lap. "A
moose is a moose, and a boy is a boy.
A moose belongs to the woods. Mac will
be the strongest moose in all the woods
of Canada. Let him be!"

Little Baptiste only shook his head. All
he would say was, "Mac is my friend.
I will find him."

So Little Baptiste forgot to find the eggs. He forgot to help put down hay for the cow. He started out alone, early in the morning.

"Have you seen my friend Mac?" he asked a fat green frog in the lake.

"Has my friend Mac been here?" he asked a porcupine in a tall tree.

"Have you seen a moose named Mac?" he asked a skunk, while standing a long way back from it. None of them said anything at all.

Then his ear caught a sound. There
was Mac, rubbing the furry skin from his
horns on a tree. Little Baptiste said,
"Hello, Mac. Where have you been
hiding? Let's take a ride."

He stood on a stump and got on Mac's back. Just then, from far out near the lake, there came a long "Honk-honk." Mac put his head up. Then he honked and honked, too.

Mac tore off into the deep woods. He ran faster than he had ever run before. Little Baptiste went flying off, head over heels. Mac didn't stop to look. He pounded away to find the honking sound. He was gone.

Little Baptiste landed with a hard thump. A big stick hit his head with a whack. His arms and legs and his face were bruised. He hurt all over. He picked himself up and went home.

His mother cried when she saw him. His father frowned and pulled on his beard. They put him to bed and gave him bread and milk. Little Baptiste couldn't eat. He whispered, "Mac was my friend."

Big Baptiste said, "When a moose is old enough, he must find his own kind. When a boy is old enough, he must find his own kind, too. We will see about that. Won't we, Marie—yes?"

Big Baptiste went out. He didn't say where he was going. When he came back he gave Little Baptiste a smile and a wink. He gave Big Marie a big nod. All he said was, "Everything is fine, Marie. You will be happy, my son, no?"

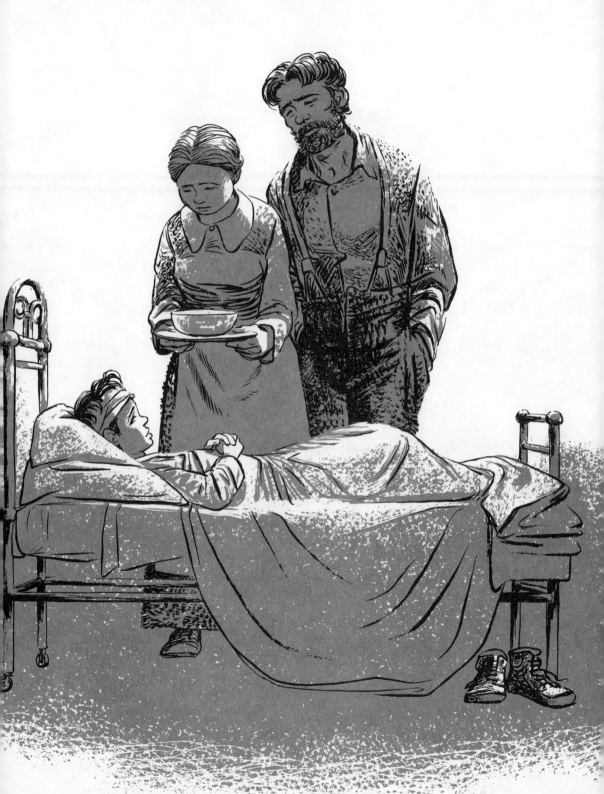

Little Baptiste wasn't happy at all.
He still hurt all over. He went to sit on
a stump at the edge of the woods. The
wind was cold. Mac didn't come. Only a
little brown mouse came out for seeds.
She looked at him and ran away. Little
Baptiste was very lonely.

The next morning Big Marie came to waken Little Baptiste early. She said, "Come, eat your breakfast. Put on your best clothes and your red cap. Here is your lunch to take with you."

"What is going to happen?" asked Little Baptiste.

"Never mind. It's a surprise," Big Marie said.

Little Baptiste got into the wagon with his father and they went up the road.

The old horse trotted along. They went
between the fields and over a bridge
across a stream.

"Look, Little Baptiste! The ducks are
flying south," said Big Baptiste.

Little Baptiste kept his head down. He
said nothing, for he was thinking of Mac.
Another wagon passed them. And then
another. Along came a car. They were all
filled with boys and girls.

"Where are we going?" asked Little
Baptiste.

"You'll find out soon enough," said his
father. He began to flap the whip a little
on the back of the old horse, to hurry
him up.

"Whoa, Napoleon!" shouted Big Baptiste to the horse.

Little Baptiste looked around his big father and saw that they were in front of the new house. He remembered that he and Mac had seen the men working on it last summer. It was a big house painted red. It had a bell on a rope over the door. A boy was pulling the bell.

"Ding-dong," went the bell. "Dong-dong-dong-dong!"

A woman came out with a book in her hand. Boys and girls jumped from wagons and cars. Big Baptiste put Little Baptiste down on the ground.

"Good-by, Little Baptiste. I will come for you later. You can go to school now. You can make some friends." Big Baptiste got into the wagon and went home.

Little Baptiste was afraid to go into the schoolhouse with the boys and girls. He stood there all alone as the others laughed and talked. He wished his father would come back for him. He wanted to run away into the woods.

A boy came over to him and said, "Can you catch a fish? I can."

"Yes, I can too," said Little Baptiste.

"Can you slide on the snow? I can."

"Yes, I can too," said Little Baptiste.

"Can you pick a pail of berries? I can."

"Yes, I can too," said Little Baptiste.

"Can you play hide-and-seek? Can you run fast? I can."

"I can too," said Little Baptiste.

The boy was silent. Then he shouted, "I'll race you to the schoolhouse!"

They ran as fast as they could to the door.

Little Baptiste got there first.

"You win," said the other boy. "What is your name?"

"My name is Baptiste."

"My name is Jack McGregor. Everybody calls me Mac."

As they walked in the door a sound came from the deep woods. It was a long, happy honk!

"That's Mac the moose," said Little Baptiste. "He has found his friends."